7/11

the HOLE in the middle

By **paul budnitz**

Illustrated by **aya kakeda**

Disney · HYPERION BOOKS · NEW YORK

This book is set in 22-point HandySans

First Edition

10 9 8 7 6 5 4 3 2 1

F850-6835-5-11046

Printed in Singapore

Reinforced binding

Library of Congress Cataloging-in-Publication Data

Budnitz, Paul.

The hole in the middle / Paul Budnitz ; illustrated by Aya Kakeda.

p. cm. Summary: Morgan was born with a big hole through his middle that gives

him a strange, empty feeling all of the time, but when his good friend

Yumi becomes ill, he finds that helping her makes him feel whole.

ISBN-13: 978-1-4231-3761-0 ISBN-10: 1-4231-3761-2

[1. Friendship—Fiction. 2. Self-realization—Fiction.] I. Kakeda,

Aya, ill. II. Title. PZ7.B8683Hol 2011

[E]—dc22 2010036236

Visit www.disneyhyperionbooks.com

For Rasika — **P.B.**

To my parents,
Yuki and Yutaka — **A.K.**

This is a story about a boy named Morgan, who was born with a hole in his middle. The hole was so big, you could see straight through him, from front to back.

Having a hole in his middle gave Morgan a strange, empty feeling, sort of like always being a little bit hungry.

Morgan's best friend, Yumi, wanted to help, so she made her favorite strawberry cake. Morgan ate it all.

No matter how much Morgan ate, the hungry feeling never went away.

"Maybe music will make you feel better," said Yumi.

So they sang and danced and played the drums as loud as they could. Morgan sang all the solos.

But music didn't make the empty feeling go away, either.

"Maybe you should just try to forget about it," said Yumi.

So they spent the day outside in the sun.

Morgan reminded himself to forget.

That didn't work very well, either.
Would anything ever fill the hole in his middle?

The next morning,
Yumi didn't come outside to play.

She didn't come out the day after that either.
Yumi's mom said that Yumi was sick and needed to rest.
The hole in Morgan's middle felt emptier than ever.

That night, Morgan stayed up late.

What could he do to help Yumi?

The next morning, Morgan got to work.

He knew just what to do.

"For me?" said Yumi. "Thank you!"

Morgan let Yumi have as much strawberry cake as she wanted. **After** all, it was her favorite.

Morgan came to visit every day.

He was so busy cheering up Yumi,
he didn't stop to think about the hole in his middle.

One day, after not too long, Yumi felt well
enough to come outside and play.

That was when Morgan realized he had forgotten all about the hole in his middle.

The hole had grown so small,
it looked exactly like
a belly button.

Morgan never had that empty
feeling in his middle again . . .

. . . unless he was actually a little bit hungry.